LUCY MOUSE KEEPS A SECRET

Story by Jane Pilgrim, Illustrated by F. Stocks May

BROCKHAMPTON PRESS, LEICESTER

AND THE POTATO PRESS, CHICAGO

Published in 1972 in the United States of America by J. Philip O'Hara Inc,
Chicago and in Great Britain by Brockhampton Press Limited, Leicester
Published simultaneously in Canada by Van Nostrand Reinhold Limited, Scarborough, Ontario
This edition Copyright © Brockhampton Press 1972
All rights reserved. No part of this book may be reproduced in any form
without written permission from the publisher
Printed in Great Britain by Purnell and Sons Limited

Lucy Mouse had always lived at Blackberry Farm.
She was born in a corner of the old stable, and
lived there with her mother and father and two
little sisters and three little brothers. She
was a quiet, kind, brown mouse, and was always
ready to help anyone.

Mrs. Nibble, who lived with her family in a
little house in the bank of the field below
Blackberry Farm, was a great friend of Lucy Mouse.
And Lucy often went down to see her and to help
her with her three bunnies, Rosy, Posy and Christopher.

One day when Lucy was crossing the yard on her
way to see Mrs. Nibble she saw a strange,
brown mouse sitting on a stone by the gate.
He smiled politely at her as she went past.

The next day he was there again, and the next
day, and the next day and the next day. Each time
he just smiled at Lucy, but on the ninth day
he jumped off his stone and walked beside her
into the field.

Now Joe Robin had been watching all this,
and he flew over to see Mrs. Nibble. "Who is
the strange brown mouse whom Lucy is meeting?"
he asked her. "I haven't seen him at
Blackberry Farm before." But Mrs. Nibble did
not know. "I will ask Lucy next time she
comes to see me," she said.

But Lucy did not go to see
Mrs. Nibble again, because she was too busy
walking in the field with the strange brown mouse.

One day Emily the Goat found Lucy busy
in a corner of her stable. She had a brush and
a dustpan and was sweeping it very clean.
"Why are you doing that, Lucy?" Emily asked.
But Lucy just smiled and went on sweeping.

Then Walter Duck met her carrying some corn
out of the barn. "What are you going to
do with that, Lucy?" he asked. But Lucy just
smiled and hurried over to Emily's stable.

And then Lucy's mother and father began
to wonder what Lucy was doing. "She used
to be such a help to me," said old Mrs. Mouse.
"But now she is too busy to think about us,
and when I ask her what she is doing,
she just smiles." "I think she must have
a secret," said old Mr. Mouse.

And all Blackberry Farm began to talk about
Lucy Mouse's secret. But Lucy Mouse just
went on smiling and being busy and going
for walks with the strange brown mouse.

Then one sunny morning there was a knock on Mrs. Nibble's door, and when she opened it she saw Lucy and the strange brown mouse standing together on her doorstep. "I want you to meet my friend Marcus," Lucy said. "He lives down the lane at Oakapple Cottage, and I hope he will soon live at Blackberry Farm." Mrs. Nibble shook hands with Marcus, and said she was very glad to meet him.

The next day Lucy took Marcus to see her family.
Marcus had a long talk with old Mr. Mouse,
and all Lucy's brothers and sisters peeped
out at him from under the straw in the stable
until old Mrs. Mouse shooed them away.

By now all the animals at the farm were very
excited. "Tell us your secret, Lucy," they
cried, as she walked towards the field with
the strange brown mouse. But she just smiled
and went on walking.

But Marcus, the strange brown mouse, stopped.
"I will tell you Lucy's secret," he said. "She
is going to marry me, and we are going to
live in the corner of Emily's stable. I am
a very proud and happy mouse."

Then all the animals shouted for joy, because they loved Lucy Mouse and were glad to see her so happy. "Three cheers for Lucy and Marcus," called Joe Robin. "And may they live happily ever afterwards at Blackberry Farm." And Lucy and Marcus smiled and waved, and everyone was happy with them.